The Weaver's Surprise

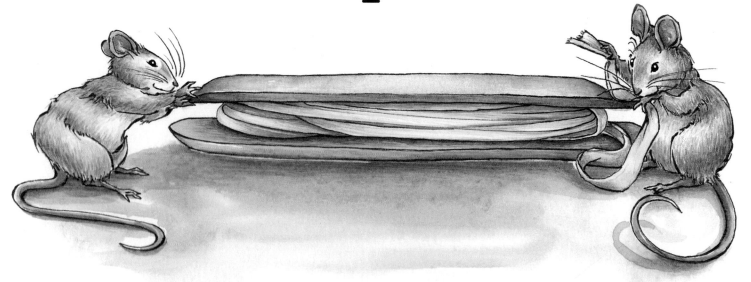

WRITTEN BY TOM KNISELY
ILLUSTRATED BY MEGAN LLOYD

STACKPOLE
BOOKS

Guilford, Connecticut

I would like to dedicate this book to my three grandchildren,
Windsor, Imogen and Jai, for they are just as curious and
sometimes mischievous as the mice in this book.
I love you,
Gumpah

To Mom and Dad. Your support made my sheep life,
weaving life, and book life possible.
Eternal gratitude and love.
ML

. . . .

Published by Stackpole Books
An imprint of The Rowman & Littlefield Publishing Group, Inc.
4501 Forbes Blvd., Ste. 200
Lanham, MD 20706
www.stackpolebooks.com

Distributed by NATIONAL BOOK NETWORK
800-462-6420

Text Copyright © 2019 by Tom Knisely
Illustrations © 2019 by Megan Lloyd-Thompson

British Library Cataloguing in Publication Information available

Library of Congress Cataloging-in-Publication Data available

ISBN 978-0-8117-3821-7 (hardcover)
ISBN 978-0-8117-6822-1 (e-book)

Printed in Selangor Darul Ehsan Malaysia December 2019

Down a long winding road, in a low-lying meadow,
an old man weaves rugs on a loom.

One day, while the old man
was weaving in his cottage,
a family of mice scurried through the meadow
searching for a winter home.

Suddenly, they stopped.
Strange sounds floated over the tall grass.

SWISH, thump, bump.

SWISH, thump, bump.

"What's that?" cried one small mouse.
"It's coming from that cottage," said another.
"Maybe someone's making dinner?" asked a third,
 very hungry mouse.
"Let's go see," said the father.

Father Mouse found a hole
in the cottage wall.
Just as the last little mouse squeezed
through, they heard:

SWISH, thump, bump.
SWISH, thump, bump.

Mother Mouse tried to cover the ears of all her
babies. The loom made such a racket that the mice
couldn't hear themselves squeak!

The mice pressed themselves into a corner behind
several rolled-up rugs and watched as the weaver
stepped on the treadles of the loom.

The warp threads in front of the weaver separated,
opening wide like a yawning cat's mouth.
The weaver threw a shuttle of rags into the opening,

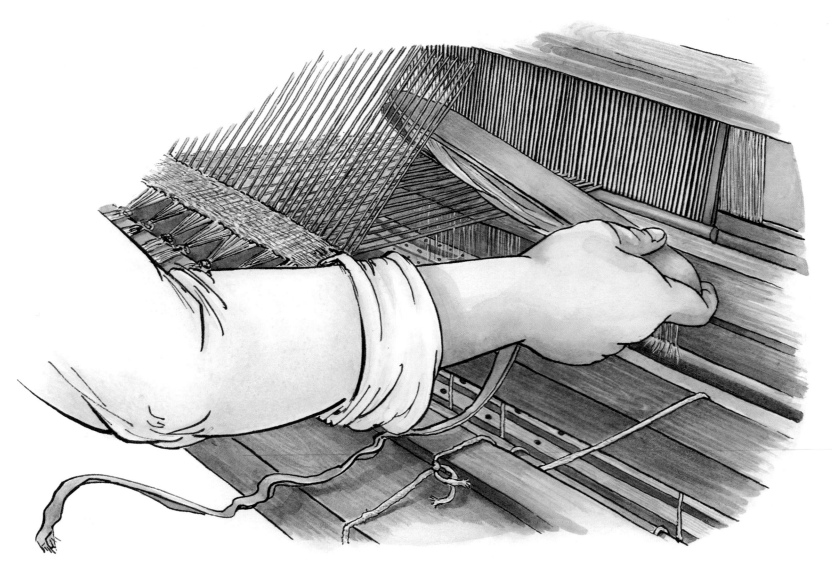

SWISH!

Then the weaver grabbed
the swinging beater and
brought it forward, very hard.

THUMP!

He did it again.

BUMP!

"That's the noise we heard in the meadow!"
"What's he doing?"

The mice looked around. Piles and piles of small
strips of rags dotted the floor. Spools of all different
colored threads filled the shelves. The weaver had
tools that spun around and around, some clicking,

some whirring. Rolled-up rugs were
stacked in every corner.
"I think he's making rugs!"
said the youngest mouse.

While Father and the little mice were staring, Mother Mouse went looking for food. She returned with paws full of nuts and crackers and crumbs of cheese. A feast!

"Oh, can we stay here all winter?" asked a tiny mouse, her mouth stuffed with cheddar.

"It's awfully loud when the weaver is working," said the father. "It might be hard to sleep with all the *SWISHING* and *THUMPING* and *BUMPING.*"

But that night, tired from a long day in the meadow, and with full bellies, the mice curled up in one of the weaver's rugs and fell fast asleep.

In the days that followed
the mice hopped from rug to
rug, searching for one that
would make the perfect winter home.

Finally Mother chose a particularly pretty
rug close to the food cupboard and tucked in a
far corner, almost out of the weaver's sight. But
this rug was very tightly woven, so it wasn't as
soft as some.

"I can fix that," said Father Mouse, and he began to chew on some of the threads. He chewed and chewed until he made a large hole, hidden in the middle of the rolled-up rug. He lined the hole with the colorful fluff made from the shredded threads.

"We could sleep here all winter," squeaked the little mice.

One day, a man and his wife came to the weaver's cottage searching for the perfect rug. The wife wanted one that had her favorite colors—green and blue and

purple—and there, in the far corner, was *just* the rug
she wanted. The weaver pulled the rug to the center
of the room. But when he began to unroll it . . .

. . . a family of mice exploded from the rug,
racing off in every direction. The wife shrieked. The
husband leaped onto a chair. Then both ran out the door!

The weaver stared at the open rug. There was
a huge HOLE in the center and a pile of colorful
fluff. This had been his favorite rug, and it had taken
him a very long time to weave. Now it was ruined and the
mice had scared away his customers.

"All that work for nothing," he sighed. Sadly, the
weaver pushed the rug into the corner.

That night the mice crept back to their rug.
"We have to help the weaver," said Father Mouse,
"but I don't know what to do."
The family sat quietly, thinking.

Suddenly, the littlest mouse squeaked, "I know! We
can weave another rug for him! I've been watching
him work and I think we can do it!"

The next morning the weaver decided to go to town.
"Maybe I can find those customers and convince
them to come back to my cottage and consider
another rug—one without mice or holes!"

As soon as he was out of sight, the mice went to work.
They measured threads and warped the loom.

The smallest mice sleyed the reed and threaded the heddles.

Father and Mother turned the beam.

The loom went

CLICK, CLICK, CLICK

as the ratchet engaged with the teeth on the beam.

Some mice wound
thread onto shuttles,

WHIR,
WHIR,
WHIR.

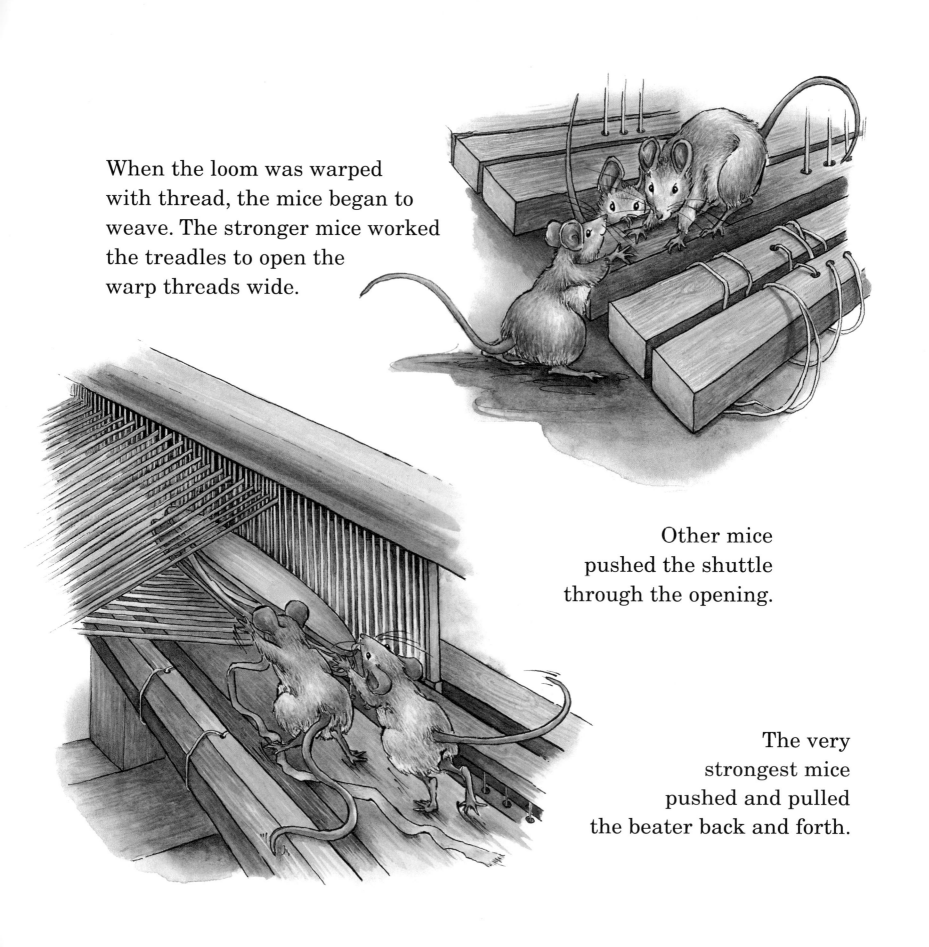

When the loom was warped with thread, the mice began to weave. The stronger mice worked the treadles to open the warp threads wide.

Other mice pushed the shuttle through the opening.

The very strongest mice pushed and pulled the beater back and forth.

SWISH, thump, bump

floated across the meadow.

SWISH, thump, bump

SWISH, thump, bump

all day long.

Together, the family wove a new rug.

In town the weaver found the man and his wife. He begged them to consider another rug. The wife was certain only a blue and green and purple rug would do, but she grudgingly agreed to go back and look again. Her husband thought he'd looked foolish leaping onto the chair, so he said he would return. "I'm not afraid of mice," he blustered.

When the weaver and the couple stepped through the cottage door, they gasped! A beautiful rug, blue and green and purple, filled the center of the room!

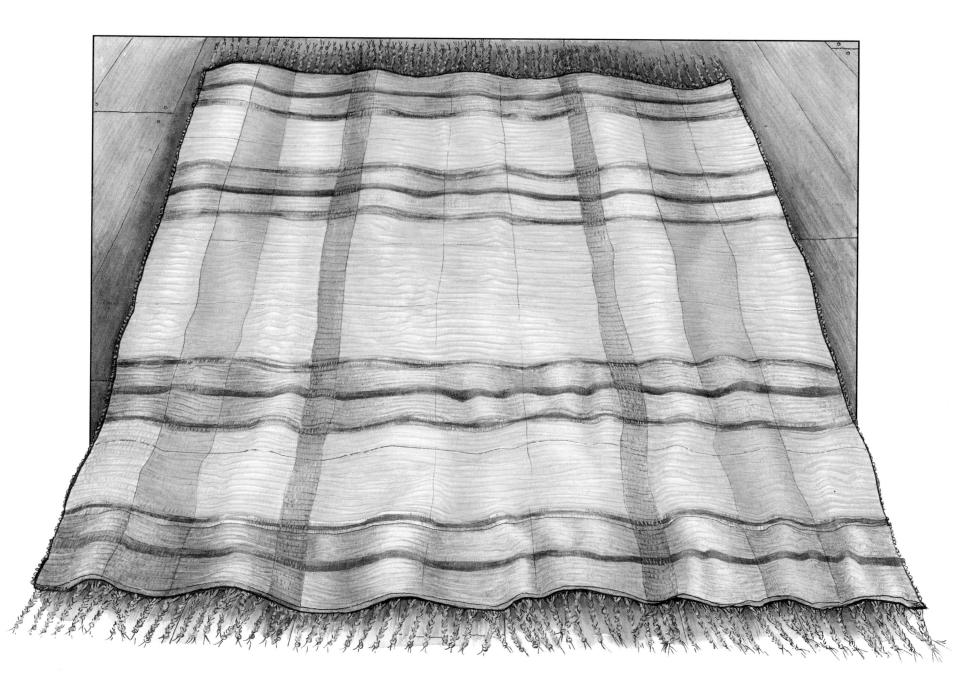

"It's perfect!" cried the wife.
"And no mice," said her husband.
The weaver was speechless.

After the couple left, the weaver looked around. A
tiny tail stuck out from behind the loom.

"Come out, come out," the weaver called softly.
"Don't be afraid. I want to meet and thank my friends
who wove such a beautiful rug. Let's eat and sing and
dance tonight, and tomorrow we'll weave rugs together!"

Bobbin winder. A bobbin winder is used to wind yarn onto a bobbin, which is similar to a spool used for thread. The bobbin fits into the shuttle and carries the yarn back and forth on the loom.

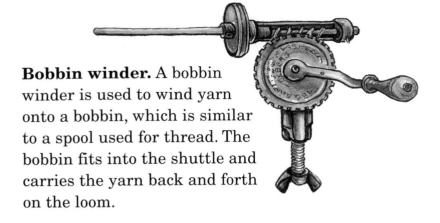

Threading hook. A threading hook is used to pull the warp threads through the eyes of the heddles.

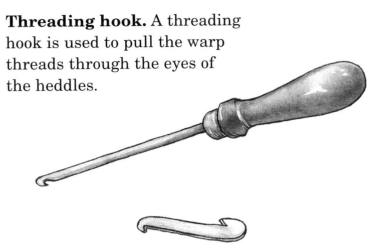

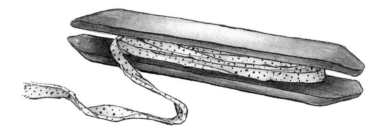

Rag shuttle. A rag shuttle is a tool that holds rag strips for weaving rag rugs.

Sleying hook. A sleying hook is used to pull the warp threads through the open slots in the reed. The reed is important to keep the warp threads aligned and in order.

Boat shuttle. This is a smaller shuttle that is used to weave yarns and thinner threads. These shuttles use a bobbin that is placed in the shuttle.

Rotary cutter. This tool helps the weaver to cut fabric into long thin strips, which are used as weft to make rugs.

Fringe twister. A fringe twister is a helpful tool that twists groups of warp ends into a tight neat bundle.

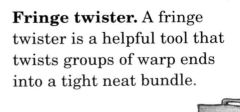

Temple. The temple is placed across the weaving to keep it from pulling inward, helping the weaver keep an even width while weaving.